We would like to dedicate this book to our daughter, as if it wasn't for her encouragement these stories would never be seen.

Sali Ann
1970 - 2019

Cottage in the Woods
The Final Visit

Black Bart Jim

&

Maggie McColl

Well, where were we, oh yes, after Danny and Vicky made their last visit to the cottage, locking it up tight, so there wouldn't be any more visitors. Vicky wrote the final part in her diary, closed it, and put it in the Strong Box at the bank. Her instructions were, 'that it not be opened until her and Danny had passed away'.

They went back to normal life on the farm and improving things as they went. They had three children, their first born was Daniel John Randon, in 1965 and named after his father Danny, and John, the man who had changed their lives. When he was young, he would help Vicky with feeding the chickens. He loved when the chicks were born each year. He would pick them up and make sure they didn't get cold, by bringing them into the house and putting them in the oven. It wasn't an oven like you have in a house today, it was called an Agar stove, it had four round plates on the top, to cook on, and a big square plate on the side, used for keeping plates and food warm. There were two warming ovens on each side and a big one in the centre for roasting and baking. The right-hand oven was usually the one Daniel would put the chicks in, to keep them warm, and he would clip the oven door open, so the chicks wouldn't be roasted by the heat of the fire. This was the normal thing to do on a farm. As Daniel grew, he would help his Dad to tend the sheep, milk the cows before they went out into the fields, and any other chores that needed doing. By this time Caroll, his sister, was coming up for two, and as little sisters do, she followed him around the farm, and that's right, got in the way, as little sisters do.

When Daniel was 4 years old, he went to the village school, Undlewood Infant and Junior School, he started in the Infants class, and at 7 he moved up to the Junior section of the school. He liked school and did very well. At eleven he had to move to the big school, at Craven, which was a bus ride away and the school was really big. There were less children in the school he had left, than in the class he was now in. He was so pleased that his friends had moved too, otherwise he would have felt lost.

At this time Caroll was 9 years old and was still at the junior school, with her little sister Sali who was 6 years old in the infant school.

Daniel had done well at sixteen in his GCSE exams and when he got near to seventeen, it was time for him to choose where he was going to go from here. So, one night he decided to sit down and discuss his options with his parent's, Danny and Vicky. Daniel said that he would like to become a farmer, like his Dad, and go to Agricultural College, and learn about all the new ways, that have come into farming since his Dad started, and then expand the farm by introducing more modern methods. Danny and Vicky thought this was a great idea, as they were not getting any younger, and Daniel would be able to take the farm over, when it got too much for them. So, they made inquiries about the different colleges, that Daniel would prefer to go to, and he applied. The following year, in the June, Daniel sat all the "A" level exams he needed, to get into University, and then it was a waiting game, as they say. They broke up from school, and in the holidays as usual, he helped his Dad on the farm.

At the beginning of August, as in most households, the excitement was rising for the students, who were waiting for their results, and to see if they got into the colleges of their choice. Well, Daniel got his letter and he was over the moon, he had passed all his exams with flying colours, and was heading for the Royal Agricultural College in Cirencester.

At the beginning of October, Daniel gathered all his clothes, books and treasures together, packed them in his Dad's estate car and his little Mini, and they drove to the students' campus, where his room would be, hoping that it wouldn't be too small for all the stuff he had brought with him. He found that he was on the top floor, which was quite a climb for his Mum and Dad. But after the second time of climbing "Everest", as Dad called it. Mum said, "I'm going off to get some shopping for you, top of the list is coffee and milk", and off Vicky, Caroll and Sali went in the Mini, as that had been emptied first.

By the time they had returned, both Daniel and his Dad were flaked out on the sofa, gasping for something to drink. Thank goodness there was a kettle as, Vicky hadn't thought of that at all. Vicky made them all a cup of coffee and she had bought some sandwiches and cakes, so they just sat around enjoying them. Thankfully, Daniel had an attic room so he didn't have to share with anyone, and he liked that idea.

The time was getting on and it was time for Vicky, Danny and the girls, to say their goodbyes. Of cause, Vicky started to cry, as you do, when your first fledgling leaves the nest. Daniel laughed and said, "I'll be home again in a couple of months, the time will fly past". So, they all said goodbye to Daniel, got in the estate car and headed for home.

In 1967 Caroll Victoria Randon, was born, her second name was after her Mother, she was such a little doll, all Mums think their babies are perfect, anyway. When she started walking, she would help Daniel feed the chickens, but he had to watch her, as she would try some of the chicken food. Daniel would shout out, "Mum she's done it again". Mum would rush out to the yard with a flannel and some water, to clean her up, Mum was sure that she had eaten some, but it didn't seem to do her any harm. Daniel thought she would start clucking like a chicken eventually.

Caroll wasn't sure of the pigs and never entered the pigsty, as they made too much noise and frightened her. But she did eventually get use to them, even though she was a bit weary at times. Daniel and Caroll would play for hours, Daniel would make up the games and he always won, boys will be boys, as they say. Time was going fast and Daniel was coming up to his birthday and he would be the first to start going to school.

After the summer was over, Daniel started school, so Caroll was on her own, well not quite on her own, not for long, as Sali came the following year. Vicky took Daniel to school on his first day, and Caroll wanted to go to school too and caused a terrible rumpus on the way home. Mum told her she had two years to wait and she would join him. When Danny came home for lunch, Caroll ran so fast to him, that her little legs couldn't keep up and tripped over, she had a bit of a cry, as she had scuffed her knees, but Dad kissed them and made them better. Vicky told him all about what had happened at school and that Caroll didn't want to come home, he did laugh, and said, "I wonder if she'll still be that keen when her day comes?"

As Caroll got to 4, or should we say, 3 going on 4, she also went to the little school with her brother Daniel and she loved it, just like him. She loved to have bedtime stories read to her, and looked at the pictures in them, Caroll would read the stories to Vicky, from the pictures, children have great imaginations at this age. As she was getting to 5 years old, her reading was getting really good, and either Danny or Vicky would sit and read to them both before they went to sleep. Eventually, Daniel would read to Caroll and when she was tired, he would get out his own boys' adventure books to read.

Caroll loved being out on the farm with the animals, she was always giving them cuddles and the lambs would follow her around, but not too far from their mums. At 7, Caroll moved up to the Junior School, Daniel had already been there a year, so she was now two years behind him. Danny decided to get a couple of ponies, and teach them to ride. It was a bit difficult for Daniel at first, as he had to find his balance. He fell off twice, but once he found out how to stay on, he was off and running, as they say. Caroll found it very easy to ride, in fact by the age of 10½ she found it easy to do a lot of things. She managed to play the recorder at school, then she went on to play the piano, then the clarinet and the guitar. She just had a knack for picking things up, with no effort.

As she was nearly 11 years old, it was time for her to join her brother once again, but this time in the big Senior School, in the next village, which was Craven. Caroll travelled on the bus with Daniel to the new school. She soon made new friends, though her old friends had moved with her, including her best friend Rio. They were really pleased to be able to stay together.

One of the best things about growing up was, you don't have to share a bedroom with your brother, Caroll was nine when her Dad decided to build onto the house, so Daniel could have his own room. That was great, as they both could have their friends over to stay, which was a bit difficult up to then. It also gave Caroll some space to do her homework and practice her musical instruments, not the piano of course, as that was down stairs in the front room.

Caroll was still helping around the farm, early morning milking had to be done first, as cows do get impatient if they don't get milked at the same time every morning. The same at night too, you take a look at a field with cows in, at about 4.30 in the afternoon, they all start walking casually towards the gate and wait for the farmer to open it. Then they make their way to the milking shed. One afternoon though, the cows were walking down the road to the farm, and a car stopped for them. The driver pulled into the side to give them plenty of room to pass. Most of the cows walked along the widest part of the road, but there were two who walked at the other side of the car, or shall we say they squeezed through, bumping the side of the car with their tummy's as they walked along. Needless to say, the driver wasn't happy. Some people call cows stupid, but they aren't really, they have a routine, and this happens day in and day out. They arrived at the shed, got to their own stalls and waited for Vicky and Caroll to start the milking. They don't need any guiding to or from the field, they know exactly where they're going, but they are a bit stubborn when it comes to, which side of the road they walk, hence the bumping of the car.

I suppose you could say they're a little like sheep. Have you ever noticed a field full of sheep, they are nowhere near you, then there is some activity going on, either in the next field or a driveway nearby? You take a look next time, they get closer and closer to the fence, one sheep starts the move and when you look around again, they're all there, just standing there and staring at you. It's very funny.

Danny and Vicky were very pleased, as Caroll, like

Daniel, had done very well in her GCSE's, and it was time for her to make up her mind what she was going to do. By this time Daniel was settled in Agricultural College. So once again it was pow-wow time, with Mum, Dad and Caroll and of course her little sister Sali, who wanted to know everything that was going on, Caroll called her a "Noisy Parker", of which she was, she just couldn't help it. She told them that she would love to be a Veterinary Doctor, as she loved animals so much, but though she would like to care for domestic animals, it was the farm animals that she would prefer to care for mainly. Vicky looked up some of the colleges and Caroll applied to Edinburgh, Cambridge and London. It was up to her now, to study hard and get the grades.

Because Caroll had her birthday in November, she was always too old for the year lower, so they put her into the year above, so she was always the youngest in the class, but it never became an issue with her. As time went on, her "A" levels were getting closer and closer, she still did her chores on the farm, but only in the mornings. She felt very lucky, as her best friend Rio Chad, wanted to be a Vet too, and they were able to study together most of the time, either at her house or Rio's. They were both very bright, and it looked like the world was going to be their oyster.

The time had come for their first exam, Maths. They wished each other luck, hugged and enter their classroom, sat down and waited for the teacher to say, "you may turn your papers over and start". After they had finished, all the students came out, hoping they had done well, some thought they had messed it up, but Caroll gave them some assurance, that it was just relief that it was all over. They all made their way to the canteen for lunch and of course discussed the exam they had just taken. The next test was 2 o'clock, so all the chatter started to die down as they began to think of the next ordeal, which was English.

The bus stopped at the bottom of the road, Caroll and Rio hugged and said goodbye, as they were both very tired after the day's exams. As she walked in the door, Sali came running up to her to ask how it went, just as she was about to answer, Vicky came into view and asked, "Well, how did it go?" "I think it went well Mum, it was a bit daunting at first, but once I had answered the first question, I felt more settled, I am feeling very tired". "Go upstairs and have a rest, I'll call you when dinner's ready", said Vicky.

It was about 6.30 when Danny came in from milking the cows and bedding them down for the night. Danny said, "Hello love, how was your day?" "Fine", said Vicky, "Caroll came in a bit tired and I sent her up to bed for a rest, you can call her when you go up for a wash, as dinner's nearly ready". "I'll do that after I've said hello to Sali". Danny carried on through to the sitting room where Sali was, "Did you have a good day Sali?" "Not bad Dad, one of the chickens was having a silly day though, it kept following me and pecking at my trousers, so I put her back in coop for a while. I went back in an hour and let her out again and she was fine". Danny said, "Good! I'm just going up for a wash and change, then I'll get Caroll, food's nearly ready". After dinner they all sat around the table chatting, Caroll was telling them all about the exams, and how she and Rio were 'very brain dead after'. About 9 o'clock Sali said she was off to bed, so she could get up early the next morning, to milk the cows. Caroll said, "Wait, I'm coming too, I'll get up and help you milk". They both gave their Mum and Dad a kiss and cuddle and raced upstairs to bed.

Next morning bright and early the house was buzzing with activity. Vicky was cooking breakfast, Caroll and Sali were out in the barn milking the cows and Danny was getting ready for another hard day harvesting the wheat in the top field. Vicky said, "Danny call the girls, please, breakfast is ready". He did and saw that they were just locking the gate to the field after putting the cows in there. They were all chatting about everything and nothing. Danny finished breakfast first and said goodbye, then Sali said goodbye, see you later and ran for the bus to go to school. Caroll didn't have to go anywhere, as her next exam was Wednesday at 2 o'clock, so she helped her Mum to do some cooking, after she had seen to the chickens, and Mum dealt with the pigs.

That afternoon Caroll phoned Rio to see if they could meet in the village for a coffee, Rio was so pleased, as she needed a break from the books. They met at Rosie's Tea Shop and had a coffee and a deliciously tasty iced bun, *'you know the naughty but nice kind'.* They talked for a couple of hours, about what they would wear tomorrow to school, about the Physics exam at 2 o'clock and all the other girlie stuff, girls talk about. Because they had to go to school at an odd time and the buses in the afternoon were a bit thin on the ground, Rio's Mum said she would take them both into school and they could come home on the bus, which was very welcome as far as Vicky was concerned and she would do the next run.

The next exams were on Monday, which was Science, and Wednesday, which was Music and finally Thursday, which was Biology. Then they could relax from the books for a while. But not from work though, farm work never stops, luckily Caroll loved the animals, so it wasn't a chore as far as she was concerned. Next week came and went. All the exams were finished, and the Summer holidays began. Daniel had come home from College, so it was all hands on deck, as they say. Vicky and Danny were happy to see all the children together again, as next term it would be only Sali at home.

That day came, at the beginning of August, when all the students at Caroll's class, were keeping their fingers crossed, some of them kept their toes crossed too, waiting for their results. The postman arrived with that all-important letter, Caroll carried it into the kitchen where everyone was waiting for her to open it. She plucked up the courage and finally opened it, she started jumping for joy and saying, "I did it, I did it, I got all "A's", she was so happy she started crying. Vicky picked up the letter and read it to everyone else, congratulations and hugs were going around the breakfast table. Caroll said, "I'm off to Cambridge for the next 5 years, whoopee!". Next, she went to phone Rio, to find out how she did, at the other end of the phone Rio said, "I passed, I got into Cambridge too". The screams of excitement were deafening in the two houses, and they made arrangements to meet, after Caroll had fed the chickens, and collected the eggs, as she had already milked the cows with Sali.

September had arrived very quick and it was time to take Caroll to Cambridge, to the student accommodation block. Caroll and Rio had written prior to this, to ask if it was possible for them to share, as they were best friends since childhood. Caroll packed all her clothes and books and other bits and pieces into Dad's big estate car, ready for the off, while Rio was doing the same at her house. Vicky had already phoned Rio's parents to see if they could all go in convoy to Cambridge, and they could all stop for lunch on the way. Caroll said goodbye to Daniel, as he couldn't go with them, because he was going back to Cirencester the next day for his final year, so they gave each other a big hug, Daniel said, "Take care and remember to study in between the drinks at the student union", and laughed.

Then they were off, they stopped at Rio's house at the other end of the village, Rio and her parents were ready, and off they went, both cars full to the brim. They had decided to stop just outside Oxford for lunch and then they would carry on. They found a nice little café just outside Oxford and stopped for an hour, then they carried on with no more stops. Danny said, "I hope their rooms aren't at the top of the house, like Daniel's was, as climbing Everest was too tiring". They all laughed. Vicky said, "Well I brought the coffee, sandwiches and cakes this time, so I don't have to go shopping" and they all laughed again.

They finally arrived, Caroll and Rio went to the office to find out where they were going to live and if they were together. They were given the address and room, and yes, they were together, so they ran to the cars all excited once again. They found the address and the girls just got out the cars and ran into the block and found their room, it was on the ground floor. Rio opened the window and shouted, "It's on the ground floor, it's lovely". Danny mumbled, "Thank goodness for that". Rio's Dad shouted, "Good, now it's all hands to the deck, you're not going to church girls". They ran back to the cars and started unloading all their stuff. When they had finished unpacking the cars, they all stopped for a break.

Both Vicky and Mary, Rio's Mum, got out the food which they had brought with them, plenty of sandwiches and goodies and of course coffee.

Vicky said that it was time to leave and make their way home, as Daniel was leaving tomorrow and they wanted to spend some time with him. Mary said, "I think we will do the same, we'll leave the girls to unpack their things and put them away". They all went down to the cars and as usual Vicky was in tears again, like she was when they said goodbye to Daniel. Caroll said, "It's OK Mum, I'll be back at Christmas, it'll soon come". Mary too had a few tears. The girls gave all their parents and Sali kisses and hugs and waived them off, as soon as they were out of site, they ran into their room, unpacked and hung-up their clothes and flunked out on the sofa, both of them pinching themselves as they couldn't believe they are actually here together.

Now, let me tell you about Sali Dorothy Randon, she was born in 1970, they gave her the second name, as a remembrance to Dorothy, John's wife and the happy times they had visiting them in the cottage, do you remember in the last book? Sali was so different to the other two, she was into everything, once she had found her feet, walking didn't exist, just running. By the time she was 4 years old, she was ready for school and so was Vicky, just to have a few hours of peace and quiet, and I think the animals were too, especially the chickens, as Sali would chase them, pick them up and cuddle them all the time. She would always be singing, all the pre-school rhymes she knew, to them.

The day came and Vicky took her to school for 9 o'clock, Sali just gave her Mum a peck on the cheek and skipped into school and never looked round, much to Vicky's disappointment. She felt unwanted, but glad that Sali was happy and not afraid of leaving Mum. Vicky picked her up at 3:30 and met Mary picking up Kisch, Rio's little sister, funnily Sali and Kisch had started school the same day, so they became best friends too, Vicky and Mary decided to go for a coffee.

They decided to go to "Rosie's Tea Shop", the best coffee shop in the village, and a treat for the girls too, while they were sitting there, Caroll and Rio were passing, so Vicky went out to ask if they would like to join them and have a drink or an ice-cream. Of course, the quiet shop became very noisy, as the children were all talking and laughing about different things. After they had finished, Mary and Vicky decided they had better go, before they were asked to leave, to give the other customers some quiet time and also to give their ears a rest. They all said goodbye to each other and went home. Vicky wondered if she was the same when she was their age, talking about everything and nothing, and laughed to herself.

Now, Sali wasn't as studious as Daniel and Caroll, she liked to sing, dance and draw. She joined the local dancing school and the local youth group. She loved it, she passed her dancing exams. Her favourite was tap dancing which she passed with flying colours and the drama side was very entertaining. Vicky and Danny went to see all the plays and musicals she was in, Kisch was in the drama group, so her parents were there too.

Time flew by and it was Sali's time to move to the big school. She was getting very excited about it. However? about nine months before, Sali was getting very tired and would fall asleep at a drop of a hat. Vicky was getting a little worried about her, and that night after she had gone to bed, she and Danny sat down and talked about it. Danny said, "Make an appointment for Doctor Davies in the morning and maybe he can give us some answers". First thing next morning Vicky rang the surgery for an appointment to see the doctor. She didn't let Sali go into school that day, as the visit to the doctors was at 10:30. She phoned Mary to ask her to tell the teacher for her. The doctor's surgery was in the village, so it wasn't far and they arrived at 10:20 and sat in the waiting room. The Doctor called them in and asked what the matter was, Vicky told him that Sali was getting very tired and falling asleep a lot. The doctor asks, "Was she drinking a lot too?" "Why yes" said Vicky. "Come here Sali, I'm not going to hurt you, I need to prick your finger, just to get some blood to test". He had this needle thing and just pricked her thumb, and smeared this piece of plastic over it and waited. "Right", said the doctor, "Sali's sugars are high, don't panic, but I'll phone the hospital now and you can take her in, are you OK with that?" Vicky was in shock, she asked, "what was wrong with Sali?", as she started to really worry. The doctor said, "I think Sali has got Diabetes and needs some tests in the hospital and then they can treat her". The doctor phoned and then told Vicky that they would be waiting in A&E for her.

By 11:30 Sali was in A&E and the doctors were buzzing around her like bees, taking bloods, putting a saline tube in her and rigging a bottle up for her urine. Then the Doctor in charge came to talk to Vicky, as he could see she was worried. He said, "Sali has got Diabetes, she'll be fine in a couple of days, when we've got her on the right Insulin. She will have to take Insulin for the rest of her life". "Is there anyone in your or your husbands' family that has it?". Vicky thought for a minute and said, "I don't know, I'll have to ask them". The doctor said, "If you want to stay for a while, that's fine, but she's going to be sleeping for an hour or so, if you want to go home, she'll be very safe with us, and there will be a nurse at the station, who can see her all the time". Vicky stayed for a little while and decided she had better go home and tell Danny and come back later, with her PJ's and washing stuff and Beauty her favourite bedtime bear.

Vicky got home and saw that Danny had been home

for lunch and gone back to the field, so she followed him up to the top field. He came over to the car and sat in, and Vicky told him the news. He was gobsmacked to say the least, "I've nearly finished this field and I'll come back to the house", said Danny. Later that day both Vicky and Danny went to the hospital, by this time Sali had been transferred to a ward. She was awake, a bit sleepy but some colour had come back to her cheeks. A nurse came to see us and said, "Her blood sugars had come down to nearly normal, which we are expecting tomorrow. We hope to teach Sali to give herself the Insulin shots, if she wants too, or she can start with an orange, which is usual. But we always leave that up to the patient, we never rush them". Then she said that if we have any questions, she will be at the nurse's station opposite, and left us to it.

They sat with Sali for a while, telling her that Caroll and Daniel send their love and that Kisch and the children at school were all thinking of her. Vicky put her washing things in the cubicle at the side of the bed, they had to leave the PJ's as the tubes would have to be disconnected first, to put them on. But Beauty was OK to be cuddled. Vicky asked if she wanted Mum to stay the night with her, but Sali said no, as the animals would have to be seen to in the morning. After about an hour, the visitors were beginning to leave and Vicky and Danny thought it was time to go too. "Goodnight, sweetie, are you sure you don't want me to stay?" "No Mum I'll be fine I have Beauty to watch over me". Danny said "Goodnight Pumpkin, sleep tight don't let the bedbugs bite". They both gave her a kiss and cuddle and left. Vicky told the nurse they hadn't put on her PJ's because of the tubes, she said that she would go and do it in a minute. They both arrived home feeling quite drained, Caroll and Daniel were waiting for us to hear any news, so Vicky makes a drink for them all, and sat down and told Caroll and Daniel all about what had happened. After that they all went to bed early, it took

Vicky hours to get to sleep as she worried about Sali. She was very temped to go back to the hospital and sleep in the chair beside her bed.

Next morning, Vicky was up and waiting for 9 o'clock so she could phone the hospital to find out how Sali was. Caroll and Daniel had milked the cows and put them out in the field before breakfast. After breakfast Caroll kissed her Mum and Dad and told them that Sali would be fine and give her my love, then she and Daniel went and caught the bus for school, Caroll told Rio all about what had happened. Danny went off to harvest the next field, but told Vicky if she needed him to call and he'd come running. Vicky cleared away the breakfast plates etc and waited to ring the hospital. 9 o'clock on the dot she rang the ward and asked how Sali was. The staff nurse came to the phone and said, "Sali had a good night, she gave herself her first insulin jab, she didn't want to waste time practicing with an orange, she just took the bull by the horns and did it. The doctor said that if it all goes well today, she will be able to go home the day after tomorrow, but not back to school for another week or two". Vicky asked the nurse to tell her she would be up later after she has fed the chickens.

Vicky went to the hospital about 10:30 to see Sali, she looked really happy and energetic too. They had taken the saline line out and the urine tube, so she could now leave the bed, but she had to measure her urine and put it on a chart that was at the bottom of the bed. She was in her glory as she was in a children's ward and some of the children were like her, some had broken their leg or arm, which they all signed. She said, "The nurse came over and gave me your message Mum, and they were laughing because they couldn't understand what the chickens had to do with coming to see me. I told them we had a farm and the cows had to be milked and taken to the field, and the chickens had to be feed and after that we had to collect the eggs". Vicky said, "I was told when I phoned that you had given yourself your first injection. How do you feel about that? You realise that is going to be a daily thing, forever don't you?". "Yes Mum, I know, three times a day, I'll be fine, it doesn't hurt". It was coming up to 12 noon and the dinner trolley was starting to come around. The nurse came over with a kidney bowl with a syringe and a small bottle, which was insulin. She watched Sali measure out the insulin, checked it was the correct measure and then let Sali inject herself. "Well done Sali, you've got it mastered", then left. She went to see the little boy in the next bed, who didn't want to do it himself, so his Mum had to do it.

Everything was going really well, Sali was coping very well with her injections, and Thursday night we all went in to see her including Kisch, whom we picked up on the way. They had so much to talk about, Danny and Vicky didn't get much of a look in. The good news was that if, when the doctor comes around tomorrow morning and everything is OK, she would be able to come home after lunch, Vicky was to phone in tomorrow about 11 o'clock to check. They were all so pleased, Kisch would tell all their friends tomorrow when she went to school.

The next morning, Vicky phoned the hospital, as asked and the answer was yes, she could come home after lunch. Sali was so pleased and so was Vicky. About 1pm Vicky got in the car and went and picked her up. She'd packed all her things in a hospital carrier bag. The nurse had given her a letter for her doctor, a prescription for Insulin, which she had to get from the pharmacy down stairs and syringes, which would last until her refill was needed. Sali said goodbye to the children in the ward, and thanked the nurses who looked after her, Vicky also said thank you to them, and left to go to the pharmacy first, then home.

About 4.30, there was a knock at the door and standing there was Kisch and two of Sali's friends, Emma and Kelli. They couldn't wait to see Sali and hear all about her stay in hospital. They wanted to know all the details in full. After about an hour of continual chatter, Sali was getting a bit tired, so they all decided to leave, but not before Sali had shown them her syringes and Insulin. They wanted to see how she injected herself, but she said, "It's not time yet, but when I get back to school, I'll show you all then, as I'll need a jab before lunch every day". Vicky was listening to this, and thought, what do children think of these days. As the girls were leaving Caroll and Daniel had arrived home from school, and were so pleased to see Sali was home.

Danny arrived home, just enough time to go and have a wash and change, before dinner. "Well then, how does it feel to be home again Sali?". "I wasn't away long, Dad, only a couple of days". Caroll said, "Come on then, show us how you inject yourself". "That's a bit morbid", said Vicky. "Anyway, we're all glad to see your home and looking a lot better than when you went in". Danny said. Later Sali went out to say goodnight to the cows, chickens and the pigs, as she had missed them, and she was sure they had missed her too. It was nearly 8 o'clock by this time and Sali was getting tired. Most people feel tired on the first day out of hospital, and Sali was no exception, so she kissed her Mum and Dad goodnight and said goodnight to Caroll and Daniel, and went up-stairs to bed.

Next morning, Sali was up, bright eyed and bushy tailed. She went out to feed the chickens but left the milking to Caroll and Daniel, as it was just a little too much for her first day out, however, she did help take them to the field. A few minutes later they heard their Mum shout, "Breakfast is ready", and they went back to the house, and washed their hands. Caroll sat at the table, while Sali went to the fridge to give herself a jab. Daniel watched her. Caroll shivered as she didn't want to see that ever again, once was enough.

Sali was not going to be sitting idly at home, Mrs Morrish, her teacher, had decided that she could do some homework, so she could keep up with her studies and not fall behind in the class. She phoned Vicky, to see if Sali was well enough to do it and sent it home with Kisch. Kisch arrived after school, and they both went up to the bedroom, to do their homework. Vicky had phoned Mary, Kisch's Mum, to ask if it was OK for her to stay for dinner and she would take her home about 7:30 – 8 o'clock. They had done their work and then decided to go and get the chickens back into the coop for the night. That was the first time Kisch had ever done that, and thought it was fun. They then went into have dinner, but first, you've guessed it, Sali needed to give herself the injection, Kisch was so pleased about that, as she would be the first to see it happen, and would be able to tell her friends about it first, as they say, *'bragging rights'*, which can be very important, sometimes.

The week soon went and Sali was back at school, her school friends were all pleased to see her and so were the teachers. Mrs Morrish said, "If you feel ill or tired Sali let me know and you can go to the nurse's room". "Now let's get down to lessons children". Lunchtime soon came, and her friends wanted to see her give herself a jab, some of them said, "I can't watch that", "Does it hurt?" "How often do you have to do it?" After Sali had explained everything to them, they all went to the canteen for lunch. It was never talked about again in school, they all just accepted it.

Sali was now 11 years old and after the Summer holidays she would be going up to the big school, where Caroll and Daniel went, and so was Kisch. The excitement of becoming the '*Big girls*' at last, as they were always little kids, to their sisters, who were already there. Now, they were one of them. The beginning of September arrived, and both of them dressed in their new unforms, met at the bus stop to go together. The first day didn't include their sisters or Daniel, as it was only new students, they were introduced to their new form mistress and shown around the school and finally their classroom. They were all given a study timetable, so they knew what lessens they would be having and at what time, and of course, lunchtime. Which was coming up in about half an hour from now and they were getting a bit hungry. They all went to lunch and then home, to get ready for the real school day tomorrow. Vicky picked them all up from school and Mary met them at 'Rosie's Tea Shop' for coffee, to hear all about how they both felt about their first day at the "Big School?"

Time after that went very fast, Caroll and Rio had left and gone to University, which meant it was Sali and Kisch's time to decide what they were going to do in the future. Sali was into the Arts, singing, dancing, but her passion was painting. She had already done some commissions for local shops, the theatre and a couple of portraits too. Her diabetes was under control and she felt very well in herself. So, when it was her turn to have a talk to Vicky & Danny, she had made up her mind, she was going to Cardiff Art College for three years, so she could pursue her future as an artist. With a proviso that she could come back home to work and maybe have the old barn, that has room for her to have a small studio in it. Before Danny could say a word, Sali said, "I will clear it and make room for myself, I don't expect you to do it Dad". Danny said, "Thank goodness, I was about to say that to you".

Next day Sali applied to Cardiff Art College and all she had to do now, was to get her grades, to be accepted. Kisch told her that she was applying to Swansea University of Fashion, as she wanted to be a fashion designer. They understood that though they would be in different towns, they would not be far away. So, all they had to do now was study and get good results.

Time had passed by so fast, that Daniel and Caroll had finished University. Daniel and his Dad, had put their heads together on modernising the way of working the farm, to make it more cost effective, not that it wasn't already, but just to make it shall we say, less hard. Like, new machinery, which will do several jobs, by just changing the tool, not just one job, one machine. After they had worked out all the finances, they decided that it was feasible, and to compensate some of the out goings, they could hire out the machinery to other farmers, when they weren't using them.

Also, they had decided that the pigs needed a bigger pigsty, so they doubled the size, and they were happy pigs and piglets, as there were six now. They also cordoned off part of the field so they could roam around a little. No changes need for the chickens, as once you let them out of the coop, they'd have food and they were free to roam anywhere. At night, when they heard you call "Feed time", they came running, and they were ushered back into the coop for the night and safety from any foxes or rats. They bought three goats and a Billy goat, as goats' milk is very tasty, they even had customers for the milk, as a couple of families had children with allergies to cow's milk but were fine with goats' milk.

Caroll had set up her Veterinary Clinic and was doing well, first of all it was the domestic pets that were coming in, but after about six months, the farmers were calling her, to see to their cows, pigs, goats etc, she was so pleased, as it was the farm animals, she wanted to specialise in. She never ignored the little animals, as she loved them too. Caroll was in her dream job and never looked back.

By the end of 1991 they were all back home, so we had a really good Christmas, to celebrate all that had happened over the last eight years. Daniel and his Dad had modernised all the farming machinery and tools, and started a hiring company, well, just a little one, but there was a future in it, as the farmers around would not have to buy machinery, that sits around doing nothing for the best part of a year, it was more economical for them to hire.

Caroll was getting a good reputation, as a Veterinary Doctor, though farmers were surprised how she coped with the big animals, as she was very small, but she knew her job and wouldn't let anything beat her, even if she needed a couple of extra hands sometimes.

Sali came home and got right down to her painting. It was slow at first with only a few local commissions. Caroll asked her if she could paint pieces for the surgery, and if she wanted, she could put a price on them and see if they would sell, which Sali thought was a good idea. Once she had done a few for the surgery, other requests started coming in, from 'Rosie's Tea Shop' for one, then a few other shops. It was getting quite busy for her. Sali started going into the woods to do some local landscape paintings, including the animals in the fields along with some of the wild animals.

This went on for a few years and she was enjoying the fresh air and all the different animals, butterflies, birds and lots more, all the vibrant colours, the shades on the trees as the sun moved across the sky. She would say to herself, what a beautiful world we live in and very few people see it, if only they could sit by me and open their eyes, they would be amazed at the variety that nature has cooked up for us. Sali would sometimes go down to the town square and paint the town hall, the grassy square with the war memorial, for the people of the town, who lost their lives in "World War 1, 1914-1918" and "World War 2, 1939-1945". She would sit and draw the people who sat for a rest on the benches, the children coming home from school. Then she would go home and paint them in the colours they were wearing.

One day Sali decided to go further into the woods, and as she was walking with her easel and paint case, she came across an old cottage. It was very old and the weeds had taken over everything, but there was a plaque by the side of the front door: "This was the Property of John Owen Henry Neil & Dorothy Olivia Estelle Whendell 1642-1685". By the time she had read the plaque and looked around, the light had started to fade and it would be no good painting it now, so she decided to come back to the cottage the next day. Sali went back many times and did some beautiful paintings, improvising with different animals, flowers and making the cottage the centre feature, with slight differences.

In the meantime, a lot of other things were happening in the Randon family.

In 1994, Caroll had met a young man named Allan Ewing. He was from Scotland, the Isle of Lismore in fact, just off Oban in Argyllshire. He had taken a position as a Doctor in the village surgery, mainly to help Doctor Davies, who was a few years off from retirement. Dr Davies wanted to make sure that when he did hang up his stethoscope, his replacement would fit right in, not just dealing with the men, women and children of the village, but also with the farming community, as sometimes the farmers needed a lot more help than just a pill. They sometimes needed stitching after an accident with a tractor etc, or setting broken bones after a fall and even a bite from an angry bull, who's having a bad day. These are all jobs that a country doctor has to deal with.

One day Caroll was just having a break, and went to 'Rosie's Tea Shop' for a coffee, she was relaxing and looking out the window, when a man walked in, and asked, "Is anyone sitting here?" Caroll looked around, and said, "No". Caroll thought to herself, that's an old line, and smiled. He said in a very broad Scottish accent, "My name's Allan Ewing. I'm the new Doctor, assisting Doctor Davies, in the village surgery". "I heard there was a new Doctor there, my name's Caroll Randon, I'm the Vet around here". "Yes, I know, I've seen you around the village, and asked about you". "Oh, you did, did you?" Caroll said, trying not to be too interested. "I've just bought a house on the edge of town, it needs some work, well a lot of work, in fact", said Allan. "Where do you live?" "I live with my family at Undlewood Farm, just up the road". Allan said, "I have to go, as I have a patient to see, I only wanted to meet you. Could I take you out to dinner one evening?" Caroll thought, then said, "OK, here's my phone number, give me a ring and we'll see. I have to go too, as I have Molly, the cow to help, with her calf". They both said "Goodbye" and went their separate ways.

About five months later Daniel asked his Mum, if he could bring a friend home to stay for the weekend. He had met Maggie at University, and they had kept in touch. Vicky said, "Yes". She thought he was going to be a confirmed bachelor. The following weekend Maggie Evans was introduced to us, she was from a village called Pontyberem, in West Wales, she was about 5 foot tall, slim, with red hair and full of bounce, and she really went down well with the family. Maggie studied different crops, and what would give the best yield each year. Vicky thought that could be a match made in heaven, and she could see how Daniel looked at her. It was reciprocal, by the look in Maggie's eyes.

Maggie came down again a fortnight later for a weekend, by this time Caroll had been seeing Allan and asked if it was alright to invite Allan over too. Vicky was enjoying this, as she was ever the romantic, and the both of them were now heading for thirty years old. Like all Mums, you always hope your children will settle down and give you grandchildren, while you're still young to enjoy them. Sali joined in with everyone and invited Kisch her best friend, Sali did some sketches, that she would paint at a later date.

It was about twelve months after that, Daniel and Maggie, and Caroll and Allan, sat Danny and Vicky down, including Sali, *you can't forget "Nosey Parker"* can you, and told them that they were getting married. They decided to have a double wedding, as Daniel and Caroll's guests would be the same people, and not many anyway, as their family was small. They would have to pick a date that was best for all, especially the animals.

Sali, Rio and Maggie's sister, Marion, were going to be the Maids of Honour and they asked Rosie, the owner, of 'Rosie's Tea Shop', if she would do the catering, including making the Wedding Cake's. Rosie was so shocked and over joyed, she nearly passed out on the spot. Rosie said, "This will be my first wedding, and it will have the best turn out of food for your guests". She was so excited. I don't think she did much else in the tea shop that day. Next, was the florist, to order the flowers for the church and the table decorations for the reception, and the most important, the bride's wedding bouquets, which of course, had to be different.

They got in touch with the Vicar, Albert Williams, and gave him the date, which was 14th July 1995, they booked the Memorial Hall for the reception. It was big enough to hold 80 people sitting down and a friend of Sali's had a band. The next thing that had to be done was the invitations and the printing, which was not so easy, as songs had to be agreed on. Obviously, the Wedding March for the entrance and Trumpet Voluntary, as their exit music, they all agreed on those. Choosing two songs for the programme, they decided to give that privilege to Maggie's mother Jean, and Vicky, and hoped they would like their choice.

Sali had decided to do a painting for them both as a wedding gift, and her thoughts were to include the old cottage in it, as it looked like it was a very happy home, she always felt happy and at ease around it. She spent many days in the forest, doing the sketches, choosing the colours and finally painting them, including the plaque by the door. In the end she was really pleased with the outcome. She then took them down to the village, as

Tony, who had framed her paintings was excellent and chose the perfect frames for the painting's.

Sali was in the studio, she had just picked up the paintings and was putting them on an easel, she would wrap them later. When her Mum popped in to see her, Vicky was dumb struck when she saw the paintings with the cottage in them. "What do you think of then, Mum"? said Sali, Vicky was so shocked, she could hardly say a word, "They're bea..ut..iful", Vicky spattered out, not knowing what to say next. Sali said, "I found this old cottage, and it was so peaceful sitting on the wall, and I felt so calm. I decided to paint it as wedding gifts, do you think they'll like them?" "Oh yes, I'm sure they will", said Vicky, starting to recover to normality. "There are so many pretty flowers around the cottage, and animals, butterflies and insects to paint", Sali said. Out of curiosity Vicky said, "Have you been inside?" "No", Sali Said, "It's all locked up, but I did read the plaque that was on the wall". With a sigh of relief, Vicky said, "I've made some coffee and Welsh cakes, so come in and have them while they're still warm". Sali loved Welsh cakes, so she didn't waste any time clearing her paints away, she would do that later.

Vicky wanted to ask Sali a lot of questions about the cottage, but was scared in case she wondered why. Vicky waited for Danny to come home, so she could talk to him about it first. Sali and Vicky sat chatting about everything and nothing, then Sali got up and went back to the studio, to finish sorting the paints out and cleaning the brushes and putting them away for the night.

At about 6:30 Danny and Daniel came in from the field, they both looked very tired, as usual dinner was nearly ready. They both went upstairs to have a shower, and Vicky said to Danny, "Call Sali on your way down". After Danny had washed, he popped his head round Sali's door and said, "Did you have a good day", Sali nodded, "I finished the two paintings and got them framed today, they look great Dad". "When can I see them then?" said Danny, "Why not now, I'll get my key, and I'll show you". "Dinner's nearly ready", said Danny. "We've got plenty of time Dad, come on". As they both went out the back door, Danny told Vicky, he won't be long, Sali wants to show him her new paintings. Vicky thought, well I won't have to explain anything, when we have a talk later.

Daniel came down the stairs just as Danny and Sali came through the back door. "So, where have you two been?" Daniel asked, before Danny or Sali could reply, Vicky said, "Sit at the table before our dinner gets cold". Danny looked at Vicky, and knew they would be talking about the paintings later. They had all just sat down when Caroll rushed in and said, "I haven't much time, Mr Wilsons cow needs help, it may be an all-nighter". Vicky straight away dished up Caroll's dinner first, everyone mumbled, "Favouritism", then they all laughed. Daniel asked Sali, how her painting was coming along, she said she hopes to finish it in a couple of days, and he can see it then.

After dinner, Caroll had gone to Mr Wilsons farm, Sali had gone to meet up with Kisch and some other friends and Daniel went for a walk down to the local pub to meet some friends. "At last," said Vicky, "did you see the paintings Danny", "Yes". "Should we say anything about the cottage, as I don't want her to get frightened", said Vicky. Danny was thinking, he said, "It's a bit of a conundrum isn't it, if we tell her it might worry her unnecessary, as we don't know if it will open up for her, do we?". Vicky said, "You're right, Sali says she's so at ease by the cottage, maybe if it does show her the open door, it won't frighten her, but show her the happiness we had visiting it". Danny said, "Let's leave it for now, and cross that bridge when it comes".

Vicky started clearing away the dinner dishes, washed up, put them away in the cupboard and made a cup of coffee for them both and a few Welsh cakes and took them through to the sitting room, put the TV on and relaxed. It didn't take Danny long to fall asleep, at least he didn't snore, like some husbands I know, Vicky thought. Daniel soon came in and Vicky made him a coffee and gave him some Welsh cakes. "You didn't say you had baked some Welsh cakes, Mum?" Said Daniel. "No, I didn't, because they would have all gone by now, remember, I know you", she gave him a look, then smiled.

Next to open the back door was Sali, Kisch and David, Kisch's boyfriend, Sali made them a drink and they sat in the kitchen chatting. David asked if he could look at Sali's paintings, as it was his Mum's birthday and he thought a painting would be a lovely gift, something different. So, they all went to the studio, Daniel asked if he could tag along, Sali couldn't refuse, but luckily, she had put the two important paintings away out of sight, after her Dad had seen them. David was amazed at the beautiful paintings and the varied scenes and shades she had used. He chose the one he thought his Mum would love and paid for it, at a reduced price, as it was a friend. They all said goodbye and would see each other soon, Kisch said, "Ring you tomorrow Sali". "Well, my dear little sister, so much talent, I should have come over to the studio a long time ago, the paintings are awesome", he gave her a hug and they walked back to the house.

The next day Sali went back up to the woods, to her favourite place, just by the wall of the cottage. She sat down in the quiet for about 10 minutes just waiting to see what would inspire her next painting. The next moment she heard a kind of click, she didn't look around, as there are many little clicks and rustles in the woods. Small animals running through the undergrowth, even a Cricket rubbing his back legs together, but it has to be really quiet to hear that in the daytime, at night they are much louder. Then there was another little sound, Sali couldn't quite put her finger on it, she turned around, and saw a rabbit coming out of the front door of the cottage. But that can't be, as the cottage is locked up tight, and there's no way in. Her curiosity got the better of her and she had to investigate how the rabbit came out of the cottage.

Next minute she heard, "Sali, Sali", and saw Mum coming through the woods calling her. She was going to mention the rabbit coming through the door, but changed her mind, as it sounds silly when she said it to herself, and left it at that. Mum asked if she wanted to come into town, and we could go for a coffee, which sounded like a good idea, she would explore the cottage another time.

They did a bit of shopping, while they were there they popped into a store where some of Sali's paintings were being shown, just to see if they were selling. Janet, the store owner came running up to them, "Sali, I am so glad you called in, as I was going to visit you tomorrow. I wanted to know if you have some more painting's, as people are loving them, six went in the last fortnight". Sali was a bit taken aback as this was such an unexpected surprise. "Well yes", Sali blurted out, "I have four, if you want to come to the studio tomorrow and pick them up". "I'll be there, about 11 o'clock if that's OK". Sali nodded, "fine". Janet said, before they were about to walk out the door, "wait a minute Sali, here", she handed her an envelope, "this is for the paintings already sold". Sali said "Thank you", she wanted to pinch herself, just to make sure she wasn't dreaming.

Vicky and Sali got into the car and drove to 'Rosie's Tea Shop', for coffee and a naughty but nice, you know what I mean, 'an iced cake'. They sat and chatted about what had just happened with Janet, Sali said "am I dreaming Mum? Is this really happening, six paintings in a fortnight?" Vicky could see the disbelief and excitement in Sali's face. She said, "Just remember Sali, you paint for the enjoyment and the beauty you create, and for the pleasure of others, not for profit, so don't let people rush you, as it will lose some of your meaning, if you understand me". "Yes Mum, I thought of that, as soon as Janet mentioned the word, *More!*". "Sali, have you got enough paintings to give Janet?" "Yes Mum, I've got plenty, but I'm not telling her that, I have been saving some paintings, as I want to have a showing in a gallery one day".

Vicky was so proud of Sali, she has done so well over the years, between studying and the ups and downs of her Diabetes, trying to get the correct Insulin that suits and the dosage. "Well, I think it's time to head home, my love", they both said goodbye to Rosie and left. They got back to the Farm at about 3.30, Sali gave her Mum the envelope with the money in it, she thought it might get lost otherwise, and went straight to the studio to sort out the four paintings and Vicky went to the kitchen, to do some baking and then prepare dinner.

The four paintings were put up against the wall for Janet the next morning, and then she began to think of the rabbit and how he managed to get out the front door of the cottage. Sali looked at her watch and thought, I have just got enough time to walk up to the cottage and have a look around. When she got there, the door was locked up tight just as it was before, she said aloud, "I must be going a bit do-lally, and imagining things, silly me". She decided that's all she was doing today and took a slow walk home. On her way, she went to see the ponies and had a talk and cuddle with them, and the pigs, but all they do is snort at you, very unconcerned. The chickens are much the same, apart from Josie, who has always been Sali's favourite, she has given her lots of cuddles since she was a little chick, Sali wouldn't allow Josie to be on the Sunday dinner menu.

When she got home, Vicky was just putting some cakes in the oven, the envelope, that Sali had given her Mum, was on the table where her Mum had left it. She opened it and there was a lot of money in it, in fact there was £470, she gasped, she couldn't believe it, Vicky said, "what's wrong Sali?" a bit concerned. Sali said, "there's £470 in this envelope, I can't believe this", jumping for joy. "I'll leave it on the table for housekeeping, I know I will get it back bit by bit, but at least you'll get the feel of it before I do". They both laughed. "Anything you want help with Mum, before I go and bring the cows in?" "No, that's alright Sali, you go and bring them in, the boys will be home soon, anyway". "Do you know Mum, when I was sitting up by the old cottage this morning, just before you came, I thought I saw a rabbit coming out of the front door. I didn't have time to look, as you came up and we went to town, but I went up to have a look before I came home and the door was locked up tight just as before". Vicky said, "it must have come around the side of the cottage, before you turned". *Thinking, was the cottage starting to invite Sali in.* "It's a really weird feeling, as I was so sure that it happened, I'll have to turn quicker next time, I wonder what's inside the cottage". "Take a slow walk up and get the cows in please dear". "On my way Mum".

Vicky had decided to cut that conversion short, so she could have time to think about it and talk to Danny tonight. Danny came in about the usual time and he knew by Vicky's face she had a problem, Vicky whispered, "we must talk later about the cottage". She then carried on making the final bits before dishing out the dinner. Sali started telling them about their visit to town and pictures that had been sold and another order of four more paintings. Danny said, "you'll be a millionaire before you're much older". They all laughed and Daniel said, "I'll be OK for a loan then".

Later, when they were on their own, Vicky told Danny what Sali had said about the rabbit coming out the front door. Vicky said, "What shall we do, Danny?" Danny could see the worry in her face, and said, "I think we had better talk to her, in a casual way, about the house, so as not to frighten her". "Listen, I'll have a chat with her in the morning, I'll make some excuse about wanting to walk up to the cottage with her". After that, Vicky made a drink for them both and they sat and watched the TV for a while, to relax.

Next morning Sali was up earlier than usual, she went out to feed the chickens and was about to start milking the cows, when Danny came into the shed. He said, "You're up bright and early this morning love, anything up?" "Nothing up Dad, I just wanted to start painting in an earlier light today". "Do you mind if I come with you, to see where you're painting today?" "Of course not Dad, I'll show you where, it's so peaceful there and quiet too, except for the birds and other animals". "We had better get these cows milked and, in the fields, then," said Danny.

They had to pass the house as they walked to the woods, and Danny popped in just to tell Daniel that he would follow him in about an hour or so. Vicky had just fed the pigs and opened the gate for them to roam in their field, she could see that Sali was OK with Danny going to the woods with her, and hoped it would remain like that. Danny helped her with her easel, which Sali loved having a helping hand. They got to the spot where Sali wanted to sit today. "This is a lovely spot you've chosen Sali", "Yes, it is, so many different ways to paint this view, the shades and colours, they change every few minutes or so". "Mum says you saw a rabbit coming out of the old cottage, yesterday, was the door open then?" "No, not when I went to have a look, it was still locked up".

Danny decided to go and have a look around the cottage, just to check it was as Vicky and him had left it, and it was. He was about to turn and go back to where Sali was, when he heard a click, where the lock was, he looked and heard door creek. At that moment, Sali was right behind him, looking at him, she said, "You've heard it too, haven't you Dad?" "What?" "The noise at the door? don't deny it, I can see it in your face". Danny made a decision to tell her the story, as if he didn't, she would just pester him and probably Vicky. "Can we sit down first and I'll tell you a story about the cottage".

They sat on the wall, where Sali had set up her easel, paper and paints, ready to start painting. Danny took a deep breath and told Sali the story of what happened to them on their honeymoon. About entering the cottage and going back to 1650's, and that's where they met John and Dorothy, who were farmers themselves. "That's where our lives changed, for the better, I might add". We thought we were in the past forever, but about six months had passed, we went out for a walk, and we were back in our own time. We were in old fashioned cloths, in the 1960's, our cloths and my car keys were back in the 17th century. We had to sneak back to the railway cottages hoping no one would see us. We introduced ourselves to the station master, who by this time was in shock at our old cloths, his name was Frank Hardcastle. I asked him if he could help us, as we couldn't get in the car, had no money of the day and I didn't have the keys either.

Frank kindly put us up in his house and we phoned home for a spare set of keys. We sat and told Frank of our experience, Frank couldn't believe they had been away six months, as he said that it was only a few hours, we found it hard to believe too. We visited the cottage many times, and helped John with the farm and your Mum was taught how to make cream, cheese, milk the cows by Dorothy, as well as many other things. When we went back through the portal, shall we say, we would find out more about John and Dorothy, and of course, we would tell them on our next visit. They were a very loving couple, and as I didn't have any parents, they became my Mum and Dad and we became their son and daughter, as their two boys had died years ago. "I think this is all for now, as I have work to do and you have paintings to paint. If the door does open for you, don't feel frightened, you can always call me or your Mum to come with you". "Wow! what a story Dad, do you think the door will open for me?" "We shall see kitten".

At that Danny said, "goodbye, see you later", and Sali said, "right you are Dad". Sali sat for a while, thinking about what her Dad had just told her and wondered if she would have an invite into the cottage and if she would meet anyone. But that would have to wait until she had done some painting, well at least two canvases. It was about 3 o'clock when the light began to change, so she started putting things away, at that minute she heard a click. Sali wasn't sure if she should call her Mum or, just have a quick look, she decided to have a little peek, being nosy as she was called. She went to the door of the cottage and it was unlocked, so she peeked in. Her eyes just couldn't believe what she was seeing, there was a roof on the house and the furniture was still there and there weren't any cobwebs, now that was weird, as even in her house there were some cobwebs. She had a good look around, there wasn't anyone there, well not at the moment. She said out aloud, "I have to go now, as I have to feed the chickens, milk the cows and have my Insulin jab, but I would like to return and do some painting of your beautiful cottage. As she turned the knob on the door she wondered if she would enter the past or be back in the present time. Gently, she turned the knob and peeped out and with a sigh of relief she was back in her time. So, without further ado, she started back home to deal with the animals.

The girls were ready at the gate to be released to walk home, their udders were full of milk as usual. Dad was going to bring Fred, the bull over, from the high field next week, so that they could have some new stock. It was the season, so Fred was in demand by the other farmers too, what a lucky boy he was, let's hope he does his job, Dad used to say.

When I got home and Mum and Dad were on their own, I told them what happened, I said I had entered the cottage and how surprised I was to see no cobwebs around the place. I told them how welcoming it felt and could understand how they felt when they first entered. Vicky asked, very nervously, "Was anyone there in the cottage?" "No, I didn't see anyone, but then I didn't stay long, just enough time to look around, but it didn't look as if anyone had been living there". "But I did ask if I could visit again, of course no one answered", Sali gave a little giggle. Vicky knew this was not going to end, as Sali was a very curious girl, so she said, "Just be aware, that you could be in the cottage for a few hours, in our time, which could be days in the cottage's time". That's all Vicky would say.

Vicky called them all to come and sit at the table for

dinner. At this time, they had one extra guest, Maggie, she had moved from Wales, as she wanted to get more involved in making sure they had the best wheat and corn in the area. Also, to get a name for herself to be on call for other farms, if they needed her. This would also bring some extra money in, in case they needed it, like the wedding, that was four weeks away. Vicky asked Maggie and Daniel, if they could add one more name to their wedding invitations, Frank Hardcastle, he was a very old friend in the village. There was a lot of chatter going around the table, between the men talking about the agenda for tomorrow and Fred the bull coming from the top field next week. When Daniel ask Sali what her day was like, she just said, "fine, I got two paintings nearly finished, I'll do the finishing touch to them tomorrow". She didn't say anything about the cottage, much to Vicky's relief.

Sali decided to go to bed early, she said she was a little tired, but in fact, that was a little white lie, she just wanted to think about, whether she should enter the cottage tomorrow morning or leave it for a few days. Maybe she needed a little more courage, in case she got stuck there and couldn't return to her own time, when she wanted to. She decided to sleep on it, and have a fresh think of it when she went to paint in the morning.

Next morning Sali got up and fed the chickens. As she was feeding them, she sat down to talk to her new best friend, Oliver the rooster. She told him all about the cottage, as she was in a dilemma on what to do, go in or stay away from the cottage. She knew he wouldn't be able to answer, but she just wanted to talk out aloud, to run it through her mind. Then after a while she said, "thank you Oliver for listening to me, you've helped me to make my mind up, I'm going to go in and see what happens, Bye, Bye, see you at tea time".

Sali was standing outside the cottage, with all her painting brushes etc, she had also brought some snacks with her and her Insulin, just in case. She went to the door, but it was locked, she gave a great sigh, she wasn't quite sure if it was a sigh of relief or sadness. As she turned to go to her normal place to paint, she heard a click and the door had opened for her. She said, "I hope you don't mind, but I have brought my easel and paints with me, as I want to do some painting, here in this time, whatever time it is". All was as quiet as a mouse, she took another look around, just to make sure there wasn't anyone living there. She peeped out the front door to see if anything had changed, and to her surprise it was late morning. She thought she had better get a move on or she'll miss the light.

She started to set everything up when she heard a noise, coming from the woods, she was a little bit scared, as she wasn't sure what to expect. Then out of the woods came this young man, he was dressed in black jacket and trousers, both a bit wrinkled and worn, with an off-white shirt, I think they use to call it 'unbleached cotton', and shoes, that could have done with a touch of polish. He was about Sali's age and very good looking, well, Sali thought so. He was surprised to see her too, he said, "where did you come from, no one ever comes here, they say it's haunted". "I come here sometimes, for the peace and quiet". "My name's James, James Rafferty, it was my father's name and my Grandfather's, and I think my Great Grandfather's too". "My names Sali, Sali Randon, but I'm the only one in my family, that I know of". James said, "whatcha doing then, I love to roam the woods, what's this then, and started picking things up and looking at them". As Sali was taking them back off him she said, "Paints, an easel and some brushes". He said, "The nearest

I come to painting is white washing the outside of my Mum's house, we do it about every three years or so, depending on the weather".

They sat there quietly as Sali started to sketch the outline of the picture. "Core, that's good, I never learnt to draw, is it easy Sali?", "Yes, if you take it one step at a time, it's practice". Sali got out a sheet of drawing paper, she had a piece of board and some pencils, she looked around at something easy to draw, and found the ideal place, it was very easy with no difficult objects. She set it up for James, "now, just take a good look at the view, imagine it in your mind, and try to put it to paper, you won't get it right first time, but it will come bit by bit". They carried on for about an hour and a half, Sali looked over at James drawing, and to her surprise, he had done very well for a first timer. He was really concentrating, as his tongue was going from side to side over his lips, Sali said, "I think you're doing wonderfully James, are you sure this is your first time?"

Sali was getting a bit hungry, so she got out the sandwiches she had made and shared them with James. "Do you live far from here?" "No, not far, just the other side of the railway station". "Do you know the station master there?" "I think his name is, Augustus Hardcastle, but they call him Gus for short, fancy calling out Augustus every time you want him, what a mouthful". Then he laughed. "Anyway, I have to go now Sali, as I have something to do for my Mum, will you be here tomorrow, as I have to finish that drawing?" "yes, hopefully I will, see you then, good-bye", "Good-bye" said James. It was time to put away her paints and stuff now and go home, well she hoped. She went in the cottage and asked if it was time for her to go, she looked outside the door and was pleased to see that she was home in her own time. She thanked the cottage and left for home.

Sali got back to the studio and put the painting she had finished away to dry properly, washed her brushes and left them out to dry ready for tomorrow. She thought she would pop into the kitchen to see if Mum was around , and to see if there were any Welsh cakes left. There was, and she ate some before anyone else got to them. Mum came in from the garden, as she picked some fresh peas, white cabbage and carrots for dinner. "Hello dear, did you have a good day?" she asked, "Yes" said Sali. "I meet a boy today, in the woods, his name was James", she thought for a few minutes, as she wasn't sure whether to say something or not to her Mum. She took a big breath and just came out with it. "I went in the cottage today and had a further look around. That's where I met James, he lives over the other side of the railway". Vicky looked at her and asked, "Did you ask him what the date was?". "No, I was a little afraid, but I'll ask him tomorrow". "Just be careful kitten, as we don't know what the outcome will be", "Gosh Mum, it's years since you called me kitten, don't worry, I will be alright, I feel the house likes me". Vicky said "OK" but with a bit of unease in the pit of her stomach.

At that Sali left, as it was feed time for the cows, chickens, pigs and goats. She thought she'd go get the cows first, as like a lot of females, they don't like to be hanging around at the gate when they have places to go. At the gate they were getting a bit noisy, because Sali was a few minutes late getting to them. The leader was Betsy, she was boss and was very moody at times if the others didn't obey her. Oh yes! they all had their individual ways, some of the young ones liked to be cuddled, and push each other out the way to get in front. Betsy led the way and the others followed her into the barn and they went into their individual stalls, ready to be attached to the milking machines. This was great, no more stool and buckets, hoping that one of the cows wouldn't kick it over. No more filling up the milk churns. Dad and Daniel had brought us into the modern age of machinery, and the milk from the cows went straight into a huge tank at the back of the shed and then was emptied by the Milk Marketing Board, once a day. Everything had to be sterilised and dirt free, which Dad and Daniel did.

Mum arrived to see if Sali was alright, which of

course she was. Vicky said, "I've brought the pigs in for you, if you want, I'll watch them, while you go and get the chickens in". "Thanks Mum". Sali only had to just go outside and shout, "Come on chooks, time for food". They started coming in from everywhere, running from all directions, it was a funny sight. Sali started feeding them as she walked to the coop and their beds, it was like the Pied Piper, but without the Pipe, just the chick food. Oliver, the rooster, lagged behind for his usual cuddle, then followed the girls into bed, and Sali locked them in for the night. She went back to the barn and Vicky was finishing off sterilising the milking pumps, they walked back to the house together, and as they got to the door, Danny and Daniel met them. Vicky put the kettle on for a cuppa, as it was only about 5:30.

At about 6:30 dinner was ready, and as usual Caroll came running in like a whirlwind, they all sat down, and chatted about their day. Daniel and Maggie were going off to the pictures in the next town, Craven. At that

Caroll got a call, Mr Rafer's horse had hurt her leg, so she phoned Allan and said she would be late, and dashed out. Danny suggested that they go for a walk, secretly hoping the cottage was open, just for a peek. So, the three of them walked up to the woods, Vicky said, "I know what you're up to Darling, I had a feeling there was an ulterior motive". "What me", all innocent looking, "I just wondered if it would be open to us again?" At that they arrived at the cottage, it looks just like the way they left it, but with a few more weeds.

"Come on" said Sali, "let's see if it's open for us", Vicky said, "have you had your Insulin Sali", "Yes Mum". with a sigh. Vicky thought, why did I say that, of course she would have had it. The door was open and they all walked in, first was Sali, then Danny and a bit wearily Vicky. Danny said, "it hasn't changed one little bit Vicky, that's weird". They sat around the table, and Sali said, "Well, it's time to tell all, don't you think now". Vicky looked at Danny and Danny shrugged his shoulders, and said, "I think we'd better tell her the story, so she's fully informed, as we weren't afraid at the time, and neither should she".

"We were on our Honeymoon in 1960, and were travelling around and saw this old station, called Undlewood. We asked this man, now known as Frank Hardcastle, if we could park in the carpark, to go for a walk, which we did. We went into the woods and found this very old cottage. We only wanted to have a look at it and see if there was anything inside. We opened the door and stepped into the 1600's, there were two people sitting there, Dorothy and John. Obviously, we were a bit shocked and so were they, we got talking to them, they were farmers, we got to know them very well. When we went to the door to leave, we opened it, but it wasn't like the place we had left, which was a bit of a puzzle. We asked them what was the year we were in? We were stunned we were in the 17th century".

"They had to give us some clothes of the time, or we would have been too conspicuous to others. We decided to help on the farm, and this is where we learned our farming skills and why we took up farming, we loved it so much, it was hard work, though. We thought we had been here for at least six months, but one night we decided to go for a walk, and when we stepped out the door, we were back in 1960. Our clothes were back in the past including the car keys and money. Our only way out of this was to find Frank and ask him to help us. We knocked on his door, and when he opened it, he was in shock. "My goodness", he said, "whatever has happened to you two?" We explained what had happened to us, I didn't think he would believe us, but he had heard a similar story when he was young.

Frank was kind enough to allow us to stay with him until our keys were sent from London and he gave us a change of clothes too, so we wouldn't stand out in the village. It was getting late and Vicky told Sali, we can tell you more another time. At that there was a knock at the door, Vicky looked at Danny and Sali looked at them, not knowing whether to answer it or ignore it. Vicky said, "You had better answer it Sali, and we'll play it by ear". Sali opened the door and standing there, was James, he said, "I saw a light and I thought I would investigate, and make sure you were alright". Sali didn't like to be rude and invited him in. As James entered, he came face to face with Vicky and Danny, now this is going to be tricky, thought Sali. "Oh! James, this is my Mum, Vicky, and my Dad,

Danny, they're visiting". James said, "nice to meet you, have you come far?" "No, not far", they both replied in unison, feeling a bit awkward. "Anyway, we had better leave for home Sali", said Danny. Praying that when they exit the door, they will be entering their own time and not staying in this one.

James was looking a bit puzzled at what had just

happened, as he knew most people in the area, but couldn't for the life of him remember them, and come to think of it, he hadn't seen Sali either, until they met outside the cottage. James then asked, "How long have you been living here, in this cottage?" Sali wasn't quite sure how to answer that, if she lied, he would know, as he knew the locals. Do I tell him the truth, that we were visitors from the future, how would he take that, would it frighten him and I would never see him again? Would he go and tell the village, all about us and the cottage? Sali was really worried that if she said the wrong thing, it might upset the karma of the cottage?

James then said, "Shall I make it a bit easier for you Sali, I know that you're not from this time". Sali was stunned at that statement and said, "How", with a puzzled look on her face. "Because, 1. Your clothes aren't in the right style and 2. Your painting stuff wasn't right either". Sali asked, "What year am I in?" "Well,", said James, "Tuesday 15th May 1913, they say there's a war coming, and I'll have to sign up to fight". "That will be the First World War". "How do you know that Sali?" "Before I tell you anything else, you have to make me a promise that, what I say, must not be repeated to anyone, do you promise?" "Yes, I promise". "I come from this date, but the year is 1991". "Wow! That far ahead, I did hear some whispers that this cottage had a lot of secrets, but this is something else". "Remember your promise James, not a word to anyone". He just stood there nodding his head, like one of those dogs, sitting on the back shelf of a car.

Sali had decided that it was time for her to go home, that's if she could? "James, I will come again tomorrow, and we can carry on painting. Over the next few weeks, I won't be able to visit every day, as my sister and brother are getting married, and I will have lots to do". At that she said, "goodbye, see you tomorrow James", and James said, "be seeing you", Sali turned and went home.

The wedding day had arrived, the 14th July 1995, it was a beautiful day too, the sun was shining, who could have wished for better. The house was bustling with excitement, it was just hectic. Caroll was floating around, as the hairdresser had arrived to do the hair for them all, Marion, Maggie's sister, had arrived from the Hotel where, Maggie, Jean their Mum, and Marion had stayed the night. Vicky and Jean had sat down and planned how everyone would get to the church, on time, which was at 12 noon.

First would be Daniel and his best man Paul, they had been best friends since junior school, they had to be at the church at 11 O'clock, with the "Order of Ceremony", which would be given out to the guests, on arrival to the church, and meet up with Allan and Gordan, who Allan had made friends with when he moved into the village.

Next would be the cars going to pick up the brides

-maids and then the brides and their Dad's. Sadly, Maggie didn't have a Dad, so Jean was going to give her away. The photographer would be waiting, when the boy's got there to start taking photos. Well, this was the plan and Vicky and Jean crossed their fingers, that it would go off as planned.

Sali said to Daniel, "Are you sure you're my brother? As you never look like this usually". She laughed. "Well, do you like it Sis", "Passable I suppose, yes! of course you are, you're my big brother", they laughed. Vicky came running in, "It's time for you boys to go to the church, or the brides will get there before you", "and don't forget the "Order of Ceremony", she shouted. "Yes Mum", shouted Daniel back, "let's go Paul, before we get more orders", and they both laughed as they were going out the door.

The cars came for Mum and the bridesmaids on time, with the second one for Danny and Caroll. But

Vicky had to check that the other car had arrived to pick up Maggie and Jean, the car was there as planned, so Vicky gave a big sigh of relief and started smiling.

Everything went like a well-oiled engine, as they say, and it all went off beautifully, the brides looked stunning and so did the bridesmaids and of course the grooms looked very handsome, in their suites. After the wedding they all went to the reception. Danny had prepared his speech, just enough to embarrass both Daniel and Caroll, as Dad's speeches do on these occasions, and welcomed both Maggie and Allan into our family, which also includes the in-laws. After a few hours of celebrating, Danny and Sali left for a little while as the animals needed seeing to, but they did return all clean and tidy.

About 9 O'clock Daniel and Maggie, now Randon and Caroll, now Ewing, and Allan, all went around their guests thanking them for coming to their very important day and hoped they had enjoyed themselves. They were about to go on their honeymoon, to different places, I might add. Yes, you've guessed it, Vicky was in tears and Jean joined her, that's what Mum's do when they're happy.

The next day, Jean and Marion were going home to Pontyberem, Vicky collected them to take them to the main station, which was quicker. They all said their goodbyes and Vicky said, "You are welcome to come down anytime for a holiday, the door will always be open for you". The train came on time and they were gone. Sali said. "Let's call in at Rosie's for a coffee, before we head home", and that's what they did.

On the following day Sali got her things and James's, things together, so they could do some painting. She got to the cottage at about 10 in the morning, set up for a day's painting and waited for James to come. She liked James but knew nothing could come of it, because of the situation. About half an hour later James arrived, he wasn't too happy. "I have something to tell you Sali", his face was very sad. "I have had my call-up papers, we are going to war with Germany, it's been on the cards for a long time". Sali thought, this is the first world war, and it was a terrible waste of human life, but it happened. She was in a quandary whether to tell James all about her, he had guessed some of it, but she had never confirmed anything. Maybe, this was a good time to tell him, as he may never come home again.

They were just sitting there painting, and Sali said, "James, you never ask me any questions, about where I'm from, you're not nosy, are you?" "I've wanted to ask many times, but I was scared in case you wouldn't come back, I know you're from a different time, I guessed the future". "Yes, that's correct, I live in the year 1991, I was born in 1970 and I'm 21 years old". They sat for hours painting and talking, Sali told him all about herself and James told her all about himself.

They met for about a week, and they would chat and paint, at this point James was getting very good at painting and choosing very vibrant colours to express his paintings. Then one day, the one Sali dreaded, the call-up papers, for James to report to the Colchester Barracks, in two days, to get ready for going over to France. Sali thought that she may never see him again. "So, you've only got two days left to finish that painting then", Sali said. "Well, I'd better get cracking", said James. They sat there for a long time not speaking a word, then James asked cheekily, "Will you miss me, Sali?" Sali paused for a minute, and said, "of course I will, you're my best friend aren't you". "Am I really, that's great, and you're my best friend too, Sali".

The day came and Sali said good bye to James, Sali felt very teary. James said, "don't worry about letters, I'll send them to my mum's address down the road, and I've told her to post them through the letter box, so you can get them. I'm not sure if you'll be able to reply though, it may be a bit tricky, in the, well the time difference, so I won't expect any letters". Sali said, "I will try my best to find a way", she then gave James a big kiss on the cheek, which surprised him, but he did give her a cuddle, and left.

Sali decided not to stay at the cottage any longer, as she felt a bit sad, she would return tomorrow to do some painting. It would be strange not having James around to chat too, she just hoped that he would be safe and out of harm's way. At this she went home and told her Mum what had happened, then she went out to talk to Oliver, you remember, the rooster, he always listened to her, when she wanted an ear to talk to.

About seven weeks had passed and when she was setting up the easel, paints and paper etc, a lady came up the lane, with a letter. It was James's Mother, she said her name was Mary, and she had brought a letter for her. Sali was so pleased and just sat on the wall and started to read it, then remembering her manners, "Oh, sorry, please sit down, would you like some lemonade?" Mary said no she wouldn't stay long. She said, "I'm so please to meet you, James didn't say much about you, but you did make a great impression on him, especially with his painting, we have a few on our walls at home, I can see you do some lovely ones too". Sali said, "thank you, it gives me a lot of pleasure". Mary then asked if she could come to visit again, as she's very lonely without James. Sali told her she was welcome. She then said goodbye and went home, at that point Sali got the letter out and started to read it.

Dear Sali,

> *We are still at the Barracks, leaning the ropes, marching, exercise, running with all our equipment, including a rifle, that weighs a ton. They haven't told us where we're going, but the boys say it's France, they were saying the battles over there are really bloody and the rain and mud never stops, so I don't know what to expect. I expect you will meet my Mum, as she is curious about you, I didn't give her any details, but I know Mum. Maybe, she could put a letter*

Sali was so happy having had a letter from James, she carried on painting with, what shall I say, like a bounce in her step, no, change that to, her paint brush. The painting was finished, just before 4 o'clock, so she packed up her things and headed for home. The cows would be waiting for her, so they could go to the shed to be milked. Sali dropped everything off in her studio and went to get the cows, and just like clockwork they were waiting patiently at the gate to go home. They started walking home and Sali shut the gate and walked behind them, no rush just a leisurely stroll, cows don't rush anywhere.

Vicky was waiting at the shed to plug in the milking cups, it didn't take long these days, as Danny and Daniel had modernised all the milking side of the farm, so no more siting on a stool, using your hands to pump the milk out. But the pigs and chickens and the two ponies, still needed to be looked after by us, but that was always an easy job, no time table, as long as it was before 8 o'clock, so they could be bedded down for the night.

After milking the cows, Mum went in to start on the dinner, as Dad and Daniel would be on their way home from the fields and Maggie was on her way home, from a wheat farmer, about 50 miles away, she had been helping him to get a better yield out of his crops and to be an organic farmer, which was going to take a bit of time.

Sali started telling Vicky about the letter she got from James, and also meeting Mary, and that she was missing him. Sali also said that she was so excited to receive the letter, so many feelings were coming to the forefront, that she hadn't felt before. Vicky knew that feeling, it's called love, but she said nothing, well not at this point, just in case. World War 1 had a terrible loss of young lives. At that point Danny came in, so Vicky was pleased not to have to continue that line of conversation.

Time carried on in Undlewood, just an easy life as it is in most small villages, nothing changes. Though there were some increases to the population, Daniel and Maggie had a little boy, Daniel Junior, in May 1997 and a little girl, Jeanie, in November 1998, and Caroll and Allan, not wanting to be left out, had a little girl, Victoria Caroll, in June 1997 and another little girl, Janette Marie, in August 1998. Vicky loved this, as they got older, they would be on the farm a lot, helping with the chickens, piglets, and the baby goats, as their Mum had twins, and they loved to help bottle feed them, they had so much fun.

Sali went up to the cottage nearly every day to paint, and Mary would come up to have a chat, sometimes with a letter and Sali would give her a letter to send James.

The War went on for four long years, but it wasn't that long when Sali went home, it was as if time stood still, just like when her Mum and Dad had gone backwards and forward to the cottage in the 1960's, remember. Sali loved getting the letters from James, and talking to Mary, she told her all about James and his growing up without a Dad, sadly, he had died of pneumonia when James was 8 years old.

One day Mary came for a visit, and Sali said, "this is for you Mary", it was a painting of James, that Sali had done from memory. His Mum was over the moon, "it is so much like him, even down to the quirky smile, Oh, thank you, thank you so much, I will treasure this". Then she asked a question, that Sali knew would come one day. "I never see you in the village, at all, and people look at me very funny, when I have mentioned you". "Does your family live near here? As no one seems to know your name". Sali quickly changed the subject by asking Mary, "could you put this letter with yours, next time you write to him please". "Yes, I'll do that tomorrow, I'm writing to him tonight". Sali said, "the light is starting to fade, so it's time to tidy up, wash my brushes and pallets". At that, Mary said that she would go home too, and asked her, if she could come down for tea tomorrow? Sali said she would.

Sali went home and told her Mum and Dad what had happened that day, and that she would have to be careful about what she said to Mary. If she told her the truth, how would she react? Sali thought, would she lose a friend in Mary? Would she be against James and I seeing each other again? All these questions were going around in her head. If she did tell her, she would have to be very gentle in the way she did it. Sali made the decision to tell her, but only if the subject came up. She told Vicky and Danny what she had decided and they thought it would be a good idea, as James would be coming home soon, as it was nearly 1919 and the war had been over about 6 months. Bearing in mind Sali was in the future, and time was much slower.

Next day she went to the cottage to do some painting, as she had one to finish for the Shop in the Craven Town, and it was promised for tomorrow, and she never liked to break her promises. It was about 3 o'clock and she packed up paints etc and walked down to have tea with Mary, she had made some scones, which were lovely, and we sat and chatted away. Then, Mary asked that question again, about my family. This was it, Sali had made her decision, she asked, "how much do you know about the cottage and its history?". Mary said, "some people say it's haunted, and that funny things went on up there many years ago, that's why people don't go up there".

"Well, if I told you an amazing story, you would have to promise to keep it a secret to yourself, otherwise I would not be able to return, either to see you or James".

Mary agreed. "I come from the future, in fact it's 1998, same month, but 79 years later". Mary had to sit down, as her legs had given way with shock. "Don't ask me how it happens or why it happens, it seems to be a time warp or tunnel, I don't know". "It happened to my parents on their honeymoon, back in the 1960's or around about there. They met a couple from the 1600's and they put a plaque on the house to remember them, when they came to live in Undlewood. I was born just down the road in 1970 and I have an older brother and sister". Mary said, "I'm still trying to get my head round all this, does James know about this". "Yes"! I nodded. "Let's have our tea and scones, my brain can't take anymore at the moment". Sali changed the subject, and they carried on chatting for another hour, before she had to go. Sali said "remember not a word to anyone, Mary", she nodded, "not a word", Mary said.

The next day Sali took some of her paintings to the Craven Town, as Janet had been asking for more, to display on the wall. As Sali walked in the door, Janet came running, "I can't tell you how fast these paintings are selling, I have 2 more orders, people are fascinated and wonder where, you get your ideas". Sali smiled a little, and thought, that if they only knew, they would think I was mad. "It's a good imagination Janet, that's all". Janet asked if she did portraits, as a customer asked her. "Yes, but it would be done as a few sittings, so I get the right texture and it looks like them", Sali said. "I'll tell her tomorrow, and give you a ring", said Janet. "That's fine, bye!", said Sali. As she left, she phoned Vicky and asked if she would like to meet her at 'Rosie's Tea Shop', her Mum said, "I've got Jeanie and Marie, (Jeanette's second name) here". "That's fine, bring them too, they can have some ice cream".

At about 20 minutes later they met in Rosie's. Vicky looked a bit harassed, as the children were very active. They both gave Sali a big kiss and hug as they met in the tea room, Rosie came over to take their order, and asked, "everything OK with you, I can see you have your hands full?" Vicky said, "Daniel Jr and Victoria were in pre-school, and ready to start infant school shortly, and these two will be going to pre-school then, thank goodness". Sali said, "yes fine", shushing them to lower the volume. "I think it's a mug of coffee and a cream cake for us, and Ice Cream for those two, thank you".

Sali told Vicky about the paintings and further orders and also about someone wanting a portrait done and they want me to do it, which she thought was exciting. Vicky said, "just watch you don't overdo it, dear, as you can't do everything in a rush, just take your time". Sali could see her mother was a bit worried, and promised she would take her time. After they had finished their coffee, they decided to return home, well, after they had cleaned the girls up, the ice cream was all over their faces and down the front of them.

Sali had decided that she would not go back to the

cottage today, and just play with the girls. She took them for a walk to bring the cows in. They enjoyed that and laughed at the way the cows were swaying from side to side, they meant the cows udders. I had to explain to them that they were full of milk, and when we get to the shed, they would have to be milked. They were fascinated when the cows went into their own stalls, Marie said "how do they know it's their stall". "They just know", I said. I hooked them all up to the machines, and they watch very closely and gave the cows some hay, in case they were hungry. After all that, we went indoors and they told their Grandmother all about it, all in such a rush, of course, they told her how funny they thought the cow's udders were swinging from side to side, their Grandmother was surprised, but had a good laugh.

It was time now to put the other animals to bed for the night, so Sali took them first to the pigs, to make sure they had food and that they had fresh hay for their beds. Marie was the real chatter box, she asked, "why do they make so much noise", she started honking like them and they would honk back at her, which made her laugh and

Jeanie thought it was funny too. They both wanted to say good-night to the cows, so we walked over to the shed, and they both went and stroked them all and said, "Good-night" to them. Then it was the chickens, there were a lot of baby ones this year, and they love picking them up and giving them a cuddle. They each took a handful of feed and coaxed the chickens into the coop, and the little ones followed their mums in.

They were just getting back to the house when Allan arrived, he wasn't doing a late surgery tonight, so he thought he'd pick the girls up early. With that, Marie and Jeanie came running to him, they couldn't speak fast enough, telling him what they had been doing. Allan said, "hold on a minute, take a breath, now one at a time, otherwise I can't understand you". Marie started, with Jeanie jumping in every now and again, if she missed anything. Vicky shouted, "Tea up! I think you need it now, after all that excitement", "That's music to my ears", said

Allan laughing. After a cup of tea and scones, it was time to go, as he was picking Victoria up from her friend's house. At that Daniel Jr came in, he'd been out in the field with the ponies, making a fuss of them. They all said goodbye to Allan and Marie, and Allan said thanks to Vicky for having Marie and left.

Next day Sali went to the cottage, just in case, you know why? She was just setting out her paints and things when, she heard a voice say, "hello, stranger". She looked up and there as large as life was James, she was so pleased to see him, she forgot about everything to do with time travel, she just ran to his arms and kissed him. James was so glad she felt the same way as him, and gave her a big kiss and cuddle back. "When did you get back? Are you OK? no war wounds", Sali looked all around him, but he was fine. "I arrived home about 10 hours ago, I knew you wouldn't be here, as it was night time, but I was hoping that you would be here now". "I'm so pleased that you are home safe and sound, James". They sat on the wall and talked about all that had happened here and in France and the Somme. It was horrifying, but Sali already knew that.

Sali started getting the easel's and paints ready, "look James you have an easel of your own now, did you do much drawing over there?" "I did, but my sketch pad got so wet with the mud and rain, that it couldn't be saved, it's somewhere out on the Somme", James said. They didn't talk for a while, they just painted and looked at the country side around them, full of peace and quiet, except for the birds singing and a few squabbles with the little foxes, trying to show who's boss. About half an hour had passed, when Mary came up with some lunch, "I thought you might be hungry the two of you". "That's just what the doctor had ordered", said James. "I hope you've brought enough for yourself as well, Mary", said Sali, "Well, yes, I did, I hoped you would ask me to stay". They all sat there just chatting about nothing and everything, until it was time for Sali to go home. They all said goodbye and Sali said, "see you tomorrow", James couldn't just say goodbye, he went up to her and gave her a kiss and cuddle, and said he'd see her tomorrow.

Mary was pleased about the outcome, but had some reservations about what was to come next. That night James did have a conservation with his Mum, telling her how he felt and telling her that he loved Sali, and he thought it was mutual. He wanted to ask her to marry him, but because we come from different times, what would the outcome be. He told his Mum he was afraid to ask. Mary said "the only way to find out, is to talk to Sali, she could be having the same fears as you, but you have to talk to each other, and see if you can come to a solution". "Anyway, it's time for bed James, just sleep on it and talk to Sali tomorrow". "You're right Mum, thanks, you know I love you and I always depend on your input". He gave her a kiss on the cheek and went to bed.

Sali was bubbling by the time she got home, she told her Mum that James had come home in one piece, and that he'd kissed her and she thinks he loves her. Vicky asked, "Well, how do you feel about that?" "Mum, my heart flutters, as I know I love him too, but where do we go to next?" "You two have to talk to each other, it's not going to be easy, but I'm sure you will work it out". Nothing more was said, as Danny and Daniel had just come in from the field, Danny said, "Johnny wants to hire Fred, as he needs some more cows for next season", Remember, Fred was the bulls' name. Then he went upstairs to wash for dinner. Danny asked if we had a good day, and we said "Yes" in unison. Apart from the usual chatter, nothing much happened that night.

Well, this was the day that Sali would have to talk to

James about their feelings and what was going to be the solution, it wasn't going to be easy for either of them. Sali didn't want to lose him, she knew that, but it was also about what he felt too. So, she got ready and make her way to the cottage, with many mixed feelings and fears too. Sali went through the cottage door and there, sitting on the garden wall was James, bright and breezy Sali said, "good morning James". He jumped up with surprise, as he was deep in thought, "Oh! good morning Sali, I didn't hear you". "You must have something on your mind then", she said. "Well, yes, I have something I want to ask you, you know how I feel about you, I love you very much, and have done for a long time. Normally I would just ask you to marry me, and hope the answer was yes! But this is different, because you live over 80 years ahead of me". "I know", said Sali, "I have been giving this some thought too, you know I love you too, I realised how much when you left to go to war". "Well,

Sali, what are we going to do about it?" "It's a bit of a conundrum isn't it, James?"

Both of them sat on the wall and started to paint in silence and thinking about their situation. After a while, Sali said, "the trouble is, that if you came to live in my time, would you age rapidly, due to the number of years ahead of you here, or would you age like me?" "If I came to live in your time, you would age as you are doing now, which is fine, but would I age slowly, as I do now, going through the time zones". "I have to remember that I am a Diabetic on Insulin and Insulin wasn't discovered until 1922, which is in a few years from now". "Mmm". They talked about this for the rest of the day, and at 5 o'clock, Sali said she would go home and give a lot of thought to what they had talked about. James was also going to go home and do the same, and tomorrow they would meet early, about 9am, and see if they could come up with a solution, so they would both be happy. They kissed and said "goodbye", they didn't want to leave each other, but they had to.

The both of them met next morning, wondering what the other had decided, so it was a very tense meeting.

Neither of them wanted to speak first, but Sali as usual, took the bull by the horns, as they say and said, "What would you say, if we carried on seeing each other, here at the cottage, as if... we were married, the only difference would be, that I would go back to my time every night. You could live here in the cottage, unless you would prefer to go home, which ever you wanted to do, I could always visit your Mum, as she knows about us. I know it isn't perfect, but is one solution. What do you think?". James didn't say anything at first, and Sali was getting a bit worried, in case she had said the wrong thing. Then he said, "I was thinking the same thing, and I am so glad we can stay together. I would go home, as

Mum would be lonely on her own, and it wouldn't affect our plans". They kissed and cuddled and said those words, that sealed their future, "I Love You".

After that they did all the things that married couples do, Sali would bring food with her from home, as she couldn't cook on the very old stove that was in the cottage. She also brought, pillows, sheets, blankets, cushions, a few trinkets and a camera, so she could take some photos of themselves and Mary & James together. Even, Sali's Mum and Dad came to visit and James went and got Mary, so they could meet each other. It was really nice that they met, and yes, we did talk about the time zone differences and all agreed that it was the best decision, so that they both could stay healthy. By this time WW2 had been and gone and it was very peaceful.

Sali went home one night, and her Mum and Dad thought they should talk, should they tell Daniel and Caroll about the cottage. It was coming to that time, when her Dad was going to hand over the reins to Daniel to run the farm and the hire equipment service. They wanted to know what Sali would want from all this. Sali said, "all I want is to come home here every night, nothing else. Anything I get for my paintings will be yours and Mums and then Daniels, shall we say, for my board and keep. If you are in agreement". Dad said, "if you're happy with that, then that is what will go into the will". Sali then said, "I think that the cottage should be kept a secret, unless it's found by accident by one of the family, as it's on our land, there shouldn't be anyone else walking there". All was agreed and that was the end of that subject.

Next day, Sali and James did some painting as usual, they had been there about an hour, when Mary came running up the road, all excited. When she got to them, she could hardly speak, as she was out of breath. "Gue..ss wh..at as she panted". "What's wrong Mum?" James was sounding very worried. Getting her breath back, she said, "James, someone wants to buy one of your paintings, that was hanging on the wall". "What did you say to them?" "I said I'd ask you first". Sali and James looked at Mary with surprise, "there you go James, you can do it, I told you that you were a good painter", said Sali. "Well, yes, Mum you can sell it, did he give you an offer?" "Yes, £50. I thought that was too much, but if that's what he wants to pay, I'll accept it, is that OK?" "Yes", said James. Mary said, "by the way, the two of you, come down for lunch about 12:30, OK", "We'll be there" they replied.

They both carried on painting, James was still on cloud 9, about his first sale, he just couldn't believe it. But when we got to his house, there was a blank space on the wall, where a painting once hung, and £50 was on the dresser for him. He gave his Mum a big kiss and then turned to Sali and gave her one too. We all sat down for lunch and Mary said, "you know Mr Brooks wants a few more paintings and I'm to let him know when they're ready for collection". "When?" James said in shock. "you'd better get busy then James Lautrec", "who?" "Henry Marie Raymond de Toulouse-Lautrec, he was a famous painter back in the 1880's". "Goodness, that was a long name, thanks' Mum for just giving me one name".

They had a good laugh at that. "Time to get back to work James, you're not the only one that's got commissions to do".

Sali thought, as painters they were doing very well in their own times, she had a few exhibitions, which did very well and James was selling his paintings too, which helped his mother to live quite comfortable for the rest of her life. Sali and James were very close and their life was very special, the time difference didn't affect their life at all. Though, Sali would have loved to have children, they knew it would be a problem, so they were very careful about it. They lived together for many years. Sadly, Mary got Pneumonia one winter and died, she was only 51, we buried her in the same graveyard as Dorothy and John. Vicky and Danny came to the funeral and put some flowers on Dorothy and John's grave, just as they did back in their own time.

By this time Danny had retired from working in the fields, it was the cows, pigs and chickens, that was his domain, the easier life now. Sadly, at the age of 70, Danny passed on. He was buried in the same cemetery as the others, James could not go to the funeral, as we didn't know what would happen, going forward in time, but he did send his sympathies to Vicky. Sali was really missing her Dad as they were very close, not that she wasn't with her Mum, but there is always something special between a daughter and their Dad.

Sali & James

Ten years went by and James and Sali were doing really well with their paintings, they couldn't take it into each other's time zone, as the currency was different, so James decided to leave all the money to the Undlewood Church when he passed on, with a few paintings, and the remainder of the paintings going to the local hospital. He had already given some paintings to Sali, which she loved and she took them home.

The next tragedy was Vicky who got a strange virus and she just couldn't shake it off and passed away at the age of 80. Again, Sali was devastated, as they had a very close relationship too. After that, Sali would go home at night, the house wasn't empty, as Daniel, Maggie, Daniel Jr and Jeanie were still at home. Daniel Jr was now a farmer helping his Dad, Jeanie was helping around the farm too, well at the moment.

Time was going on to fast for Sali's reckoning, as James was coming up to 75, and he was not doing too good. It was winter and he really got sick. Sali was worried and decided to ask Allan if he could come and look at him, of course she had to tell him the story of how they met, he was surprised to say the least. He did come though, and said he had Pneumonia, and was sorry that it had gone too far, he prescribed some medicine, and said he would go and pick it up for him and bring it back. But sadly, James passed away before Allan came back, Sali was in tears, they had been together over 50 years. Remember, this was in James's time, which went much faster and was only 1971. The present time that Sali lived in was much slower and her year was in 2021. They had a loving and caring life, which they worked out between the two time zones. The problem now was, how was Sali going to bury him without too much fuss.

Sali tidied up the cottage and went down to the Doctor first, then the Minister, who had buried Mary, his mother. She had her story nearly worked out and she'll play it by ear for the rest. The Doctor came up straight away and phoned the funeral parlour and they came and took him away. Sali told them that she would pop down tomorrow to make the arrangements and fill in any forms that needed filling in. She decided to leave the Minister until tomorrow, as it was getting late and she wanted to go home.

As Sali was walking home, all in tears, Allan was coming towards her, with the prescription for James. As he reached her, Sali cried, "he's gone, the light of my life is gone". Allan said, "he's not gone, you'll always have him in your heart, you know that, don't you, and one day you will meet again". "So, each night, look up in the sky and say hello to a star and that will be James shining down on you". They both walked back to the house in silence, Allan came in for a coffee, which Sali made, and they had a chat about the cottage. Allan was stunned that she kept this secret all these years, with only Vicky and Danny knowing about it. He asked, "what are you going to do now?" "I'm going to clear it out of all the 21st century stuff, leave the rest, and close it up for good, as it was James and mine, little piece of paradise, that we shared for over 50 years". "I have written about my life with James, just like Mum wrote about her and Dad's experiences, back when they got married, they found the cottage on their honeymoon". Allan was surprised at that too, wondering how they could keep it quiet all these years.

Allan said he would have to go now, as the children would be coming home from school. "Will you be alright Sali? I could stay a bit longer if you needed me". "No, I'm fine, thanks for stopping with me and seeing to James". "Allan, you won't say anything to Caroll, will you?", "She wouldn't believe me anyway, Bye". At that Allan left, feeling a bit guilty about having to go. As he got to the gate, he could see Maggie driving up to the gate, and waved. Maggie waved back and shouted, "everything OK?" "Yes", said Allan "all's fine", knowing that it wasn't quite true.

The next day Sali went to the cottage and then to the Funeral Parlour to arrange and pay for the funeral. Then she went to the church to arrange the service and hymns, for the following Tuesday. She told the Minister that James wanted some of his paintings to go to the church and any money left, after paying for his funeral. The following Tuesday James was laid to rest next to his mother Mary. There wasn't many there, but the sound from the hymn singing was beautiful and I was so pleased that he had a good send off. I made arrangements for the Minister to come and collect the paintings and also gave him the money that was left, which he was surprised about and very grateful, as it was over £1,000. He did ask what I was going to do about the cottage, I told him I would be locking it up, as I was going away for a while.

Over the years Sali put her whole soul into painting and in a lot of them, just off centre, there would be a young couple, and you could see they were very much in love, and yes, you've guessed it, it was Sali and James. As Allan had told her, she looked up at the stars every night and said "hello" to the brightest star, and she felt James at her side.

Thankfully, Sali got on alright with all the family, and it was a happy house. Sali would spend most of her time in the studio painting as she had lots of commissions for paintings and portraits. By the age of 65 she did start to slow down, she had to go for an eye test and found out that she needed glasses. She didn't like that much, as she had her vanity to think about and her looks. She did come around one day, as she couldn't find a certain colour paint, that was right in front of her eyes, so she had to give in and wear glasses. So, she chose a really flash pair, so her vanity wasn't too frayed.

When she was about 70, she started to feel unwell, Sali had always had her Diabetes under control after the first year, when they had to change her Insulin, which they called the *'Honeymoon period'*. And yes, if she had a bad cold, it was always a bit harder to keep it under control, but to her it was no big deal. So, Sali decided to go to the Doctor, and yes, it was Allan she saw. He took her vitals and decided to send her to hospital for more checks.

She went for a full overhaul, they took a lot of blood,

she asked the nurse, "have you left me any blood to live on?" They both had a laugh, then it was the scan, blood pressure etc, Sali told Doctor Andrew, "I should have brought my easel and paints with me, to paint you all busying around me". The Doctor said, "You realise this is the Royal treatment Sali, we haven't had anyone so famous in this hospital before". Sali burst out laughing, "You're joking, I'm just a country painter, I'm not famous". Doctor Andrew was very proud of the two local painters, he said, "We have two local painters in this area, one died a long time ago and you. People have graciously donated the paintings to the hospital, or left them in their wills". At this point Sali was scared of asking who the other one was. You know when you get that feeling inside of you, well, Sali had that same feeling inside her.

Doctor Andrew said, "I tell you what, while we're waiting for the results, let's take a walk around and I'll show you these paintings, that we are so proud of". As they walked into some of the wards, Sali saw some paintings by her beloved James, but couldn't say a word, but inside she felt so proud of him. All she could say was, "they are beautiful". They were paintings he had given his Mum, and when she died, he gave them to the local hospital. "Excuse me! Are you Sali Randon?" "Yes, I am", she seemed to recognise him but wasn't sure. "I knew your Mother and Father, I met them first when they were on their honeymoon, they stayed with me for a while, but that was back in 1960. I am over 100 years old now and I know a story, that may shock you". Sali quickly said, "I don't think so, Frank, is it?" Frank was gobsmacked, he didn't know that anyone else knew this secret. "I tell you what Frank, can I come in and talk to you tomorrow, I can't today as my tests will be completed now". Sali waved goodbye and left.

"You knew Frank then?" "Not really, my parents did, it seems, so I said I would visit him tomorrow for a chat". "He'll like that, as at his age all his friends have gone before him". They got back to the Doctor's office and all the results were waiting for him. They sat down and he looked through them, "well, you seem to have a little infection, not serious if we treat it now". "Unfortunately, at your age, Diabetes can play up and we need to take extra care with you, as you have had a trouble-free life up to now, but at 70 your body isn't as strong as it was when you were younger. Well, that goes for all of us, so I'm going to give you some antibiotics to get rid of the infection and I want to see you, once a month for a check-up, OK". "Can't Doctor Allan Ewing do it?" "No, I want to see you myself, I know Doctor Ewing and he's an excellent doctor, but I would prefer to see you myself". Sali said, "goodbye, and I'll see you next month".

The next day, Sali was very excited to visit Frank, to hear his story, she caught the 1 o'clock bus to Craven Town hospital, and went straight to the ward where Frank was. "I'm glad you came, Sali, I wondered if you would", "I was intrigued at what you knew about the cottage". Sali continued, "I do know about the time differences and what happened in 1960, with Mum and Dad, they had to tell me as the cottage opened up to me too". "People living in Undlewood thought it was haunted and never went near it, but your parents found it one day and saw the other side of it. The door unlocked and allowed them into their world, the owners John and Dorothy, treated them as their family, and left the land to them back in 1685, That's how you live on a farm and a happy one I understand too". "Yes, it is a happy family". "Have you had any experiences at the cottage? Mmm, I can see by your face the answer is yes". Sali started a bit nervously, as she still wasn't sure what to say, or even how much to say. "It did invite me in too, but it was 1913, just before WW1, I did a lot of my paintings there, as the place was so lovely, with different colours and shades". Frank said, "and?" Sali went on, "I met a young man there, his name was James Rafferty". "I knew him, nice boy, lived with his Mum, widow I think, and?". "We fell in love, we never married as it wouldn't work, with the time difference and all, but we were together for over 50 years, until he died. I miss him terribly, even after all these years, but one day we will be together again, so until then, I will look to the stars and say 'Hello' to him". Frank and Sali chatted for about an hour and a half, then Sali waved goodbye and went home. She did visit him a few times after that for chats.

About a month later Frank passed away at 101, and the whole village turned out to give him a roaring farewell, he was placed next to his Mum and Dad, I told him to tell James to watch out for me when I come. Which turned out to be a long time.

My paintings were still selling well, but arthritis had now set in, and my hands were getting sore from holding the paint brushes, but on a happier note, two nieces and a nephew had settled down and had lovely partners. Only

Marie was still single, she was an Interior Designer and a very good one from what I was told. She had bought some paintings from me to hang up in her houses and flats that she designed, which gave me a lift.

Sali was still visiting the hospital once a month, but time was taking its toll, she was now the ripe old age of 85 and things were starting to go wrong, as they do at her age. Sadly, just after her 86th birthday she peacefully passed away in bed. Allan asked if he could make the arrangements for the funeral, and the family agreed to leave it to him. Sali's instructions were to be cremated and the ashes to be scattered in the front garden of the cottage. Allan arranged all this, and a little more too, he took some of the ashes to scatter them over James's grave later, so they would be together forever.

The turnout for the funeral was like a festival, there were hundreds there, from Craven Town, the shops had shut down where she had her paintings showing. I think the whole of the village of Undlewood turned out too, the church was full to the brim with standing room outside. The singing was awesome and everyone thought that she would have been proud of the send-off. The family couldn't believe the crowds that turned up, from all walks of life. They didn't even know how famous she was, and I don't think Sali ever realised it either. It was only the family that went to the Crematorium for a private service.

About five days later, Allan picked up the ashes during his lunch break, he opened the box and took out two tablespoonfuls of the ashes and put them in a pot, and put them on his desk. He took the rest to the farm, at the weekend, when all the family were together. They walked up to the old cottage. They all stood holding hands, as Allan scattered the ashes and said a prayer.

Here we stand to scatter your ashes, where you were happy and content. May you never stop painting this beautiful

The next day, Allan quietly took the ashes that he had separated from the rest and scattered them over James's grave, and said, "here you are James, you and Sali are back together again at last, she loved you right to the end".

Allan walked back to the farm, but on his way, he picked up two books, which he left in the surgery for safe keeping. He had retired many years ago, but asked the resident Doctor Thomas if he would allow him to keep these books locked up here, until he wanted them or his death. He took them up to the farm and laid then on the table. "I was asked to keep these safe until Sali passed, then I could give them to the family. One was your Mothers diary and the other is Sali's diary, she gave me instructions to give them to you, to read after she was gone, and here they are".

Caroll asked if he knew what was in them, Allan said, "I haven't read them myself, but Sali did tell me about some of the contents. I would suggest that you read your Mums first, then Sali's, it will help you understand a lot of things". "I'll make some food for us all, and maybe after we can sit down and start reading Mum's book".

After reading both books, they all sat back in amazement, wondering if this was true or fantasy, they decided to put it away and let the family pass it down to the next generation and so on, but before they did, they all walked outside and into the front garden, and stood in a circle, looked up to the stars and said, "Hello, to you all in the stars, someday we will meet again".

Together again my love